CAMP
BIG PAW

CAMP
BIG PAW

Story and Pictures by
DOUG CUSHMAN

Harper & Row, Publishers

For Sally Doherty
and Camp Waka-ja-Waka

I Can Read Book is a registered trademark of
Harper & Row, Publishers, Inc.

Camp Big Paw
Copyright © 1990 by Doug Cushman
Printed in the U.S.A. All rights reserved.
1 2 3 4 5 6 7 8 9 10
First Edition

Library of Congress Cataloging-in-Publication Data
Cushman, Doug.
  Camp big paw / story and pictures by Doug Cushman.
      p.   cm.—(An I can read book)
  Summary: Cyril and his cabin mates Ben and Obie run into trouble
with the camp bully during Field Day contests at Camp Big Paw.
  ISBN 0-06-021367-1 : $. — ISBN 0-06-021368-X (lib bdg.) : $
  [1. Camps—Fiction. 2. Bullies—Fiction.] I. Title.
II. Series.
PZ7.C959Cam   1990   89-26867
[E]—dc20   CIP
                                                       AC

CONTENTS

1. CAMP BIG PAW   7

2. BIRDHOUSES   15

3. CANOE RACE   21

4. SWIM RACE   27

5. BIG PAW   35

6. CAMPFIRE   53

1. CAMP BIG PAW

Ben and Obie arrived

at Camp Big Paw.

"Welcome to the Junior Camper

Field Day!"

said Mr. Badger.

"I am your leader.

The contests for the camping badges

will begin right away.

We will have loads of fun.

"This year we have a new camper,"

Mr. Badger said.

"Everyone meet Cyril.

He will stay in Cabin Five

with Ben and Obie.

Get all your gear in your cabins,"

Mr. Badger said.

"Then we will meet

in the craft cabin

for the first contest."

Ben and Obie showed Cyril

to Cabin Five.

"Dibs on the top bunk," said Obie.

"Dibs on the bottom," said Ben.

"I guess I get the cot,"

said Cyril.

Cyril unpacked his bag.

"Is that all you packed?"

asked Obie.

"Where is your sleeping bag and

your Junior Camper pocketknife?"

"I did not know

I needed them," said Cyril.

10

Just then a weasel stuck his nose

in the cabin.

"So you are the new camper,"

he said.

"Just remember,

I win all the badges

in *this* camp."

12

"Who was that?" asked Cyril.

"Nigel Snootbutter," said Ben.

"Don't pay any attention to him."

"He is just a bully," said Obie.

"I hope camp will be fun,"

thought Cyril.

2. BIRDHOUSES

"For the first contest
every camper will build
a birdhouse," said Mr. Badger.
"The best birdhouse
will win the badge."
"I have never built a birdhouse,"
said Cyril.
"We built one last year,"
said Obie.
"It is easy."

"Ouch!" cried Cyril.

"I missed."

"I think you put the walls
upside down," said Ben.

"They look the same to me,"
said Cyril.

16

"How do the birds get inside?"

asked Cyril.

"They go through the hole, silly,"

said Obie.

"What hole?" asked Cyril.

"Oh, Cyril, you forgot

to make the hole," said Ben.

"We can help you make one."

"Should I paint my birdhouse red or green?" asked Cyril.

"How about both?" said Nigel.

"Let me help."

"Watch out!" cried Cyril.

SPLAT!

"Much better!" said Nigel.

"Finish up your birdhouses,"

said Mr. Badger.

"It is time for lunch."

"I do not think I like camp,"

Cyril said to himself.

19

3. CANOE RACE

After lunch the campers

gathered on the shore

of Lake Big Paw.

"The first canoe to the finish line

wins the race," said Mr. Badger.

"Ready ... set ... go!"

"We are not moving very fast,"

said Ben.

"Cyril, you are paddling

the wrong way," said Obie.

"Turn around."

"Watch out!" said Ben.

"Sit down!" cried Obie.

SPLASH!

"Sorry," said Cyril.

They turned the canoe upright

and paddled to the shore.

"Did you have a nice swim?"

asked Nigel.

"I would like to punch Nigel

in the snoot," said Obie.

4. SWIM RACE

The next contest

was the swimming relay race.

"We can win," said Obie,

"if we pass the baton quickly."

Mr. Badger raised the flag.

"On your mark ... get set ...

GO!" he cried.

Ben dove into the water

and swam as fast as he could.

He handed the baton to Obie.

Obie swam hard to Cyril.

"Grab the baton!" Obie cried.

"We are ahead!"

Cyril reached down

to grab the baton.

SPLASH!

"Oops! I lost the baton," he said.

"Hurry up and find it!"

shouted Obie.

"I got it!" said Cyril.

He swam to the finish line.

"I made it," Cyril cried.

"Here is the baton."

"Did you lose this?" asked Nigel.

"We lost because of me,"
Cyril said sadly.

"You did your best," said Obie.

But both Ben and Obie sighed.

5. BIG PAW

The campers lined up

for a long hike.

"Here are maps to Picnic Rock,"

said Mr. Badger.

"The first cabin

to reach Picnic Rock

will win the hiking badge."

All the campers

rushed up the trail.

"Try not to get lost,"

said Nigel.

He ran ahead.

Nigel turned the trail sign

to point the wrong way.

"Ha! Now they will never find

Picnic Rock," he said.

Ben, Cyril, and Obie
arrived at the sign.
"The map says
we go this way here,"
said Ben.
"But the trail sign says
we go *this* way," said Cyril.
"The map must be wrong,"
said Obie.
"We go this way."

They climbed over logs
and through prickly bushes.
"Are you sure you know
where you are going?"
asked Cyril.
"Of course," said Obie.
"It is just a little farther."

"I think we are lost,"

said Ben.

"We should have been there

by now."

"We will never find our way home,"

said Cyril.

"We will starve

and be eaten by wild animals."

Suddenly a twig snapped.

"What was that?" asked Cyril.

"Probably a wild animal,"

said Obie.

"Maybe it was Big Paw,"

said Ben.

"Who is Big Paw?" asked Cyril.

"Big Paw is a big, hairy monster
with bright yellow eyes,"
said Ben.
"He lives in the woods
and eats Junior Campers
who are lost," said Obie.

"I think he is behind that rock,"
said Cyril.

"We are only teasing you,"
said Obie.

"There is no such thing
as Big Paw."

45

Suddenly they heard a noise.

"*Ooooo. . . .*"

Two big yellow eyes

glowed from a tree.

"Help!" yelled Cyril.

"Big Paw!" cried Obie.

"Ooooo..." came the sound again.

"Look," said Ben.

"It is only an owl."

"Wait," said Cyril.

"I hear another noise."

"It is over there," said Obie.

They followed the sound.

"It is Picnic Rock!" cried Obie.

"And the other campers

are already there!"

"We lost again," said Cyril sadly.

6. CAMPFIRE

Everyone hiked back down the trail

to the camp.

"Well, jolly campers,"

said Mr. Badger,

"what a fine day we had.

Now I will hand out

the camping badges."

"He might as well give them all

to me now," said Nigel.

"I know I won them all."

"For the winner of the canoe race,

Cabin Twelve," said Mr. Badger.

"That is *my* cabin," said Nigel.

"I did not think

we would get *that* badge,"

said Ben.

"For the best hiking and swimming,

Cabin Twelve again,"

said Mr. Badger.

"Eat my dust," said Nigel.

"And the camper

with the best birdhouse,"

said Mr. Badger,

"Cyril from Cabin Five!"

"That's me!" said Cyril.

"But that birdhouse was a *mess*,"

said Nigel.

"It was the most colorful

and the most popular

with the birds," said Mr. Badger.

"How could it be the most popular?"

asked Obie.

"Look," said Mr. Badger.

56

All the birdhouses were hung

in the trees.

But only Cyril's house

had a flock of birds

around it.

"The birds know

which house is best,"

said Mr. Badger.

"What is your secret, Cyril?"

"I saved my pie crust from lunch
and put it inside,"
said Cyril.
"I wanted to welcome
the birds to their new house."

"You used your head,"

said Mr. Badger.

"A good Junior Camper

always uses his head."

"Hooray!" all the campers cheered—
everyone except Nigel.

"Just wait until next year,"

he said.

"Okay," said Cyril,

"then we will win

all the badges!"

Ben and Obie shouted, "Hooray!"

63

That night the campers

cooked supper over a campfire,

and Cyril told a story

about how he used his head

to trap Big Paw

with a piece of pie crust.

JE   VALHALLA
Cushman, Doug.
Camp Big Paw $11.89

COPY 2

DUE DATE   NOV 24 1997

MAR 19 1999		
MAR 30 1999		
MAY 07 1999		
JUL 30 1999		
AUG 19 1999		
OCT 14 1999		
NOV 16 1999		
		FEB 23 1999